HALF A HEARTBEAT

SHIVAM

Contents

Preface

This isn't a fancy story like all the others you have read until now, but the flavours of reality and feelings will be there.

This is my first time writing a story. This is a real story of two characters showing the one-sided relationship of Samir towards Gunika. The story is narrated in the third person view with dialogue exchanges between Gunika and Samir. Please keep this in mind while reading, as I am writing from Samir's point of view. I might not be able to describe what Gunika was feeling at that instant exactly, but I tried my best to lay it out for you. Samir and Gunika's names are used for identity protection purposes. I hope you will respect that.

This is a story of college students; placements are coming close, and COVID-19 time is there; that is, 2020. When everyone was at home, the dire situation started.

Acknowledgements

Thanks to my Gunika for coming into my life and my dearest friends who were there for me when I was lost.

CHAPTER ONE

Encounter

October 2020, in the middle of the afternoon, Samir, as usual, was worried about placements and jobs as they were near; worries were coming into his mind, and looking outside the window, *"So time is near; let's see what's gonna happen"* he said to himself.

Suddenly he picked up his phone and scrolled through his contacts to discuss his worries; suddenly a thought struck his mind: *"Let's contact the placement team member."* After checking through, he typed the message while thinking in his mind to Gunika, the placement team head.

That was the turning point in his life; a guy who never felt any feelings in his life was unaware of how his life was going to change.

After waiting for some time, the phone rang, and here's a message from Gunika.

Started with a normal chat regarding a query, suddenly Samir felt, "I think I should ask her how she is doing, actually," and asked her about her life, with this first stage of this incomplete one-sided love journey started.

CHAPTER TWO

THE FLUTTER WITHIN ME

Days went by, and Samir and Gunika started talking about general things; not even a single day did they miss talking to each other. As it was Covid time, so both Samir and Gunika were at their homes. As days went by, placements were near, and then Samir thought about building a college project. At that time, he contacted his college friends to work on this, and then he decided to include Gunika too. As both were good friends now, so all, including Gunika, started working on the project.

> *"Sometimes life takes a turn where we don't know what's wrong or right or whether we are on the right thing or not and in that situation,, you should be calm and go with the flow."*

Samir went with the flow, and now both Samir and Gunika are talking late at night for project discussions and doubts; they become more comfortable with each other.

One night, sitting beside the lamp, Samir was waiting for Gunika's call, but with every single beat of his weary heart, he was waiting for Gunika's call, but she didn't answer all the calls and didn't call. That day Samir understood what a void feeling is, even though this was a simple thing he was worried about and feeling missing.

> "*They say sometimes when you regularly talk with someone, without that person, you feel a void.*"

That's what Samir was thinking, and with this flickering thought, Samir slept.

"Why does even this matter to me? What's happening to me? I might be feeling something for her, right? But how is that possible? I never met her in person, even pre-COVID, when offline classes were there" Samir reluctantly asked himself these questions, and with each thud of his heart, thoughts were compounding.

CHAPTER THREE

Being Afar

"Maybe I should try to avoid checking whether it's a feeling or just a coincidence." With this thought running in his mind, he decided to avoid Gunika to check his theory.

For the next sixteen days, there was no talking between them; Samir tried his best to avoid Gunika's call. Sadness was lying in his heart about what he was doing, but within these days he came to know how much he liked Gunika, but he didn't know the reason.

"Maybe this is real; I like her, yes! That's it," murmuring to himself, Samir smiled, and with this thought, his void was filled.

That was the time Samir understood,

"With distancing, true love intensifies; when you let that person go, then only do you feel true feelings towards that person."

CHAPTER FOUR

HURTFUL REALISATION

"Sometimes to test someone we unintentionally hurt them at a certain point even when we think we are doing right."

The same thing Samir did, upsetting Gunika with his actions, and to cover it up, he lied to her again that he was busy. One thing that was different in Samir's case was that he was sincere about his feelings while he felt sorry, and Gunika felt that, and she forgave him.

"He isn't wrong. Maybe he was really busy". This must be the thoughts going through Gunika's mind while forgiving Samir.

But she wasn't aware that Samir was already in stage two, the feelings phase, where unknown things happen to you; the person whom you feel this about is like oxygen for you. This same thing was happening to Samir.

Samir was happy with how things were going, but one thing that was making his chest heavy was his feelings, about which Gunika was unaware.

"When you have feelings for a person and that person doesn't know about it, it's like you are fighting an unknown war where you are only expecting the results of your efforts."

The same thing was going for Samir, who was facing a war he wasn't aware of, and he wanted to get out of that unknown feeling of losing.

CHAPTER FIVE

An Echo of My Soul

"I have to get out of this black hole where all of my actions and energy feel like going nowhere according to my expectations, and the reason is she doesn't know how I feel about her. Let me open up with her. Yes, that's what I should do," he murmured again to himself.

He messaged Gunika, as it was midnight and he was desperate to tell Gunika about how he felt, and after conveying his feelings towards her, he sent that message to her, switched off his phone and slept. But a small lingering feeling was going in his mind. *"What if she read these messages now only? I should check."*

He picked up the cell phone and switched it on, and yes, there it was, Gunika's message: *"What's this? Is it a joke?"* She was confused about what to say.

"No, I mean that. Let's talk in detail about yesterday on the call," Samir suggested.

"Okay, sure." That was her last reply, but Samir was now not able to think straight, as tomorrow was the day when he would confess his feelings to Gunika, the girl he had feelings for. It is a huge day, with thoughts popping up in

his mind. He didn't remember when his eyes were relaxed and closed down, and he went to sleep.

The next evening Samir called Gunika again to confess.

"Hey... so how did you feel?" He asked straight away and waited for an answer.

"About what?" Confusingly, Gunika asked.

"About my feelings, I conveyed over chat that I like you," he exclaimed.

"Oh, I thought you were joking around, and again, one thing is there; it can be just overthinking, as we usually talk too much to someone. It happens in some cases, but that's not a real feeling; with time it disappears," she explained.

"No! That's not it; I was also thinking the same, but now I am confirmed. I tested it my way, and I am sure I have feelings for you," Samir exclaimed with an uneasy feeling.

"Okay, but I don't think so. It's real, and how can that be? What do you like about me?" she said.

"I don't know what I like. Your eyes are beautiful, but I know that's not a reason. Your nature is so good, but that's not a reason too. I don't know; I just feel like that," Samir answered.

Puzzled with the answer, Gunika asked, *"So what now?"*

"Please think it over and tell me yes or no, and if it's a no at this instant too, please tell me," Samir said.

"It's not like that; it's like I never thought of going into a romantic relationship," Gunika answered.

"Take your time; I won't bother you," Samir told Gunika confidently.

CHAPTER SIX

IN PERSON

"People usually think it's easy to give time and expect that other person will tell them instantly or in some time but life doesn't work like that, there are so many things from other person's point of view which have to considered by them at the time of making a decision. One should have patience if they tell someone 'Take your time'"

That's what Samir didn't get properly; Samir, filled with impatience and worry about the answer, was asked in one way or another to Gunika about the answer. For some days, the same story was going on. Gunika tried her best to avoid answering as she was not prepared.

Months went away, and finally, the day has come: back to college for the final year exam. Samir was worried about exams and other academics but was happy simultaneously that he was going to meet her, the one he usually talked to over calls.

"When you are in love and meeting your partner you create multiple scenarios in your mind you

will do to make sure it won't look awkward or to do something to make them sad, that's an unconscious mechanism which usually in the case of lovers, it's not like you are being a different person it's just a gesture to make yourself assure that you are taking care of your partner."

And on the first day, he got ready to meet her, and finally, when he was standing with his friends on a walkway path, somebody called, "*Gunika here!*" With every clanking-voiced step, Samir's heartbeat was also increasing, and finally, here she was, the most beautiful lady in Samir's world: Gunika was in front of him. Gunika reached her hand out to every person there for a greeting, but Samir was left out. Samir felt bad. "*Maybe it was due to the mask I am wearing, but wait, everyone is wearing the mask... then why not me? ...* "murmuring in his mind, standing blank, Samir said, "'*Hello, Gunika,*" and Gunika replied, "*Hello*".

That was an unexpected situation, a scenario Samir never thought of, though it was a trivial greeting but meeting in person after this long with his friend, he was not expecting something like that, and then Gunika went with her friends, and Samir, standing there for a few moments, also started moving. As exams were going on and finally only the last two exams were left, Samir again felt uneasy about all the encounters with Gunika, where she greeted other members of the project team normally, but there was some hesitation in his case. Continuously this thought was running through his mind, and he suddenly picked up the cell phone and called her.

"*I want to talk about something; are you free?*" Samir asked.

"*Yes, sure,*" Gunika replied.

"*I know this is very trivial, but I have this thing going in my mind: when we first met in person at Pathway, you greeted all but not me. Why? Just asking, as this is pestering me again and again, sorry,*" Samir said.

"*When? Oh, that time it was due to a mask, I think. I am sorry if you felt bad,*" Gunika answered.

"*Okay...*" Samir replied.

CHAPTER SEVEN

SCRIBBLE DAY

Samir was not satisfied with this answer, as all the others were also wearing masks, but he didn't want to drag it out, and then they started talking about scribble day when we college friends would part ways and then write all our feelings and some fun writing on each other's t-shirts. And Samir slept that night by burying that thought and starting a new day and waiting for scribble day.

And after the last two exams, finally, the scribble day was here. Samir was happy, and all were indulged in writing and creating fun moments, some were sitting alone, and in this crowd, after getting some of his shirts scribbled with writings from his friends, Samir was on a mission to find Gunika, as he wanted to make this day memorable with her, because always he wanted to make as many memories with her as possible. And here she was, surrounded by her friends, and she called him, *"Samir, here!"* and Samir smiled and said, *"Coming!"* and then they wrote the wishes on their tees. They didn't want to write any unnecessary things; in this case, not even Samir, as he knew how college days were; rumours are faster than bullet train speed. So it was general wishes they wrote, but Samir was happy; he was really happy with that writing from his most loved person.

Gunika usually teases Samir by cracking some jokes, so she teases him while saying *"Write on Komolika's tee."*

Samir smirks and says, *"No! Don't joke around"*.

After that, they continue with other friends, but as in every group, certain friends romanticize every boy-girl relationship. Samir was having some of them, and they wrote, *"I love you, Gunika,"* on his shirt. *"Stop it, guys, please!"* Samir requested. But bashful friends completed their task, and here it was a bold-marked sentence. Samir grabbed his jacket and wore it to make it not visible as he didn't want to make things awkward for Gunika, he hurried back, and when he reached the room, he saw that scent; he felt a slight unknown feeling, and then he packed that shirt, which was a treasure to him more than anything.

CHAPTER EIGHT

DOORS TO NEW HORIZON

Final placements were here some days after project week, and due to the intense downfall in the market because of Covid, every single effort was looking not good enough; jobs were low, and the situation was dire, but fortunately, most of them got jobs; Samir also got a job after trying hard. But more than that, Samir was worried about Gunika, as she had multiple offers, but none of them were satisfactory. She was having an interview for the same company as Samir but for a higher role, as she cleared the promotion exam.

> *"When you are in love with someone, you don't care about situations, you want to be there for them for moral support, and you often don't know what's happening. But one thing is sure, you genuinely want the best for that person even if that person hurt you. And that's my friend is paradoxically the best thing."*

Samir having the same situation called Gunika.
"Hey, any update on your interview?" Samir asked.

"Not yet, but I'm not sure if I will be able to clear it or not", Gunika replied in a low mood.

"Don't worry; you will clear it. I believe you. If there is anything I can do, let me know," Samir reassured her.

The conversation goes on, and finally, Samir can lift away some worries from Gunika's head. Not surprisingly to Samir, Gunika got the job and started working as it was Covid, so all companies were following work from home, which allowed Samir and Gunika to talk over calls, usually not that frequently due to their respective work.

CHAPTER NINE

MEET AND GREET

Feb, 2022. Samir decided to visit college, and Gunika's home was also in the same city, so Gunika asked him to visit or meet for the first time. Samir went to her house and met her parents, confused with his thoughts as multiple things were going on in his mind. Gunika and Samir enjoyed their talks, and they were happy, but sometimes we don't realize when we unintentionally hurt someone. The same thing Samir did while conversing, as Samir's feelings took control, and Samir asked her about her feelings, which made Gunika awkward.

> **"Sometimes it's better to keep your feelings to yourself and think if it's a place to speak up about that if we don't want to lose someone precious to us as a single mistake can do a lot of harm."**

Gunika, awkwardly dodges the question, and then Gunika's mother joins them, and this sweet little interaction comes to an end after a few hours. While going back, Samir realizes and also apologizes to Gunika for the same. Gunika must have felt bad at the time, as she just wanted to enjoy some moments with her friend, not get awkward.

"There is no such thing as perfection, not in a person or love, we all are students learning to cope with feelings, The same is true in the case of Samir, he was learning from his mistakes, and he was happy that he was making progress for his loved one."

CHAPTER TEN

A Sip of Bitterness

Samir usually does something to make Gunika feel special, though never reciprocated over those efforts, as Gunika was not sure and needed time, I guess. But Samir was not familiar with one thing at that time.

"Humans are very simple, if they don't open up at a particular time then compounded emotions will burst out, and they will be difficult to control. To maintain that stable temperament should be the main goal."

That's what Samir understood once he made a significant mistake. Unhappy and agitated by the same response and actions from Gunika's end, Samir got fed up, and when you are fed up and negative, you are just one step away from being a toxic human. That's where we all have to control ourselves by putting a leash on our overthinking, which in general creates a clouded mental state.

"Where are you?" Samir called Gunika and asked.

"I am just outside for a small tour with my friends; I will call you later," Gunika answered.

"So they are friends; then who am I? Why are you ignoring me and my actions, which I am doing to show my sincerity? See, I am not complex, and I don't like it. I say to the face what's in my mind, "Samir said furiously.

"See, we will talk later as I am in the car; there are so many people around me," Gunika messaged him sharply after hanging up.

"See? You don't care," Samir messaged.

Samir called her multiple times, as they say.

"When you are having unstable thoughts and being toxic, only you can stop yourself with small thinking and self-questioning 'Is it needed?'"

But Samir didn't get it at that instant, and here comes a situation when he behaved like a toxic human. He called Gunika and told her, *"I don't care about you, and so on"*.

CHAPTER ELEVEN

PHASES OF LOVE

"Sometimes all you need is some peace to calm yourself; anger can burn some relations."

And here Samir did the same by doing this. He realised that what he did was wrong, and when Gunika was back from the trip, he apologised to her. In these past days, Samir relentlessly thought about the things he did and why he did them and had an enlightenment that made things clear to him.

"I love her... That's why I went to those lengths, and things were going too fast from my end; I didn't have any time to think it over..." Samir said while talking to himself.

"Love is not a single episode, but a series of episodes, starting with a small feelings phase then a jealousy phase, and then the toxicity phase, and if you go above the toxic phase you will find yourself at ease as now finally you have taken the step forward towards true love where you truly live for your partner and love your partner selflessly. This stage is tough to achieve

as we usually place a great emphasis on our egos as a human. But to achieve this one has to leave that. "

Samir was feeling something similar; he finally understood that love is not about keeping someone under control or keeping them in a cage; rather than this, you will feel at ease every time they smile with joy and not control them.

After this realization, Samir finally reached the final stage of love. He called Gunika and again apologized and made up for his mistake, but Gunika was upset this time; she made it clear that he should never do it again and not do any unnecessary things again.

"But gifts are different. As a friend, I am sending them, and I promise when you feel awkward, I will stop," Samir promised her.

Samir continued his efforts to limit making sure Gunika didn't get awkward. He wrote and sang a sorry song for her to make up for his mistake, did things but also made sure to understand the limits as he was also evolving.

CHAPTER TWELVE

FAMILIAR INTENTIONS

Everything was going smoothly, though Samir was indirectly showing his sincerity about his feelings. No matter what he did, Gunika never reciprocated those feelings, but now Samir was changed; instead of feeling down and overthinking these trivial things, Samir patiently waited. As for Samir, Gunika's presence and happiness were the only things that mattered. They started to share a more friendly bond. Gunika was genuinely a nice human, not in the eyes of Samir due to his feelings, but in general, she was the ideal girl.

Thursday evening, while walking and talking to Gunika.

Samir generally asked, *"Is everything alright? You sound down"*.

"Yes, just things going on in my mind," Gunika replied.

"Tell me; maybe by sharing it, it will help you," Samir suggested.

Gunika told him about her male best friend, whom Samir was familiar with, that he was behaving strangely and she was feeling distant. Samir suggested to her *"Talk to him, as with talking and sharing your worries with that person, you will sort out things, I believe"*.

"*Yes, I will try to,*" Gunika replied.

Two days later, Gunika told Samir that everything was okay now with his friend and her and said thanks for the advice. Samir was happy to help her.

> **"Naturally, at a certain point, women know the true intentions of women, and men know the true intentions of men"**

Samir has the same feelings about Gunika's male friend; he is uneasy about it but not in the wrong way. He was sure that that guy was generally good.

JUSTIFYING GESTURES

At the end of December 2021, Samir and his friends planned a trip, and while on the train, and roaming around the city, the only thought in Samir's mind was about Gunika.

Sunshine was kissing his forehead on the train while he was writing his feelings about Gunika while writing; his heart was pounding like every single word was drowning in his heart, and tears in his eyes made his friends worried. Joking about something that went into his eyes, Samir dodged the question. After a 3-day trip, on the last day, while purchasing gifts, he purchased a simple dream catcher for Gunika, as Gunika told him strictly no expensive things, but for Samir, this was enough. But the main issue for Samir was how to give it to Gunika, as she mentioned no gifts, only on particular occasions, and that was also not required.

"When you feel something for someone, you want to give all happiness to them even small ones, and in one-sided what's the drawback, you

find reasons to justify your gestures. That's the hardest part."

Samir called Gunika, *"Hey, how are you? I have got a simple gift for you; will you accept it?"* bluntly said to Gunika.

"What's the need for that?" Gunika asked.

"Umm... I am buying for all my friends; that's why..." Samir answered.

"But I don't need any gift," politely declining, Samir Gunika said.

"*Sometimes we men also don't know their true intentions, sometimes the girl doesn't want to accept the gesture not because she is not being respectful or understanding, but due to her parent's trust and societal norms.*"

That's what going on in Samir's mind, and he understood.

"Well, this is a small one, so worry not; it's not something expensive, and I genuinely understand what your worries are. You don't need to worry about it, as I am giving this present to a friend. Please understand that friendship is more important to me, so please don't worry and overthink," Samir reassured.

After hearing all the points of Samir, Gunika accepted. Samir was happy about it but also sad to think about when he could give a present to her as a lover, not just a friend; sometimes it's hard to cope.

That's how this trip with his friends comes to an end.

CHAPTER FOURTEEN

DISTANCE BETWEEN US

For the next few months, Samir talked to her while properly working on his projects and priorities and tried to sincerely show his worth and true feelings. There were times when he was watching the ceiling, alone, praying to God and manifesting that she should be healthy.

One day, while talking to Gunika, Samir noticed something different about her tone and told himself, *"It might be my delusion,* "that was the end of the day.

In the next conversation, Samir noticed the same thing: Gunika was ignoring him at a certain level and not giving that much reaction. At this moment, instead of making his justifications in his mind, he asked her directly, as he didn't want to create any complex situation.

"Hey, I am noticing that you are ignoring me and feeling distant, and giving me fewer reactions. What happened?" Samir confronted.

"Nothing is wrong; I am being myself; maybe you are overthinking," Gunika replied.

"But I noticed and felt like that," Samir again said to get an answer.

"Then I don't know; it's your problem," Gunika told him.

For the next few conversations, this topic comes again and again on certain days. While the discussion was going on, Gunika told Samir, "You fabricate talks; I know you".

Dumbfounded, Samir was not able to think and said, "But how? I am being myself; it's not like I am making anything up, and what's wrong with you for the past few days?" Samir exclaimed.

"Don't makeup things; I am not a child and understand all things," Gunika replied.

This conversation went on for some days, and in those days, all Samir could think was, *"What's the reason for her behaviour Is it due to me or my mistake? But I improved myself and apologized for the mistakes I made and made up for that, then why?"* guilt-filled, Samir continued murmuring to himself in his mind with his wet eyes.

> **"When guilt comes by, a person always thinks maybe it's due to me even though that person is not sure if it's his fault or situation."**

Samir apologized to her if he did something wrong and murmured to himself, *"It might be due to the situation, so it's not a mistake of any of us, but I apologize "*.

Samir till now was not able to think of any reason for this but reassured himself by saying *"All is good; that's the matter,"* and happily continued his work.

CHAPTER FIFTEEN

CONFRONTING AGAIN

Next month, Samir and two of his friends planned a small trip, and on the way back from the trip, they stayed in Gunika's city and explored some unexplored places. Wearing tees and loose pants, walking on the street to enjoy night views, and posting pictures on social media as we all usually do.

Gunika called Samir, *"Hey, are you still in the city?"* She asked.

"Yes, why?" Samir asked.

"Let's meet then if you are not busy," Gunika said.

"Will let you know after some time," Samir answered.

Samir wanted to meet Gunika, but due to past events, Samir was unsure whether to meet her or not. Will she be hurt by it? And he was more worried about his feelings as it was piled up due to unanswered questions. But finally made a call to meet her. It was a normal meeting, and she brought a small gift for him. He was touched by this gesture and was talking about general things, and the meeting came to a nice end. Then after this, Samir parted ways with friends as he planned to visit his cousin's house in a nearby city.

On reaching the house while waking at night, Samir felt uneasy. *"It's been a long time since we had a conversation about the answer to my proposal."* Samir was unaware of Gunika's thinking as his questions were answered, and he wanted some answers as the feeling of losing her was overtaking his thoughts.

Samir, feeling that he should do this, called Gunika. *"Hey, it was a nice meeting today. I have something to discuss with you. Are you available for a conversation?"* ..Samir asked.

"Same here. Okay, sure," Gunika replied.

"I know we've already discussed this thing, but I wanted to know your answer regarding my proposal," Samir exclaimed with a heavy heart.

"When a person has unanswered questions he is like a pressure cooker, filled with lots of emotions and when the lid is off, that person speaks all things in his or her mind bluntly."

The same was the case for Samir.

Adding to it, Samir said, *"I know I might be lacking at some point, not having that much success at the moment, and not an ideal fit too, but I assure you I will improve for myself and you. I will try to get everything done, so worry not; I am serious about you, and I am damn serious. Please, if it's possible, just for once give me a chance; I am not taking it as a fling; I want to marry you".*

Samir wasn't sure if what he did was right or wrong. For him, getting answers is the prominent thing for that moment.

"I understand, but this makes me too awkward. I try to understand that I respect my parents' decision, and I am not into any love marriages," Gunika answered.

"So will you just go with anyone just like that, spending your whole life with that person, whom you don't even know, and how that person feels, or does that person even have true feelings for you?" with a soft voice and low energy, Samir asked.

"I guess meeting that person for some days and then coming to a decision about whether yes or no is enough," Gunika answered.

"Okay, I respect that, but why not me?" Samir asked the final question, as every person at some point asks.

"It's just I don't see we have a future together; that's why," Gunika said in a low voice.

"And please, now I am enough awkward; can you give me some time? I won't be talking to you for some time," Gunika added.

"Okay ... sure ..." Samir not knowing anything anymore... not understanding anything, it felt like his heart shattered into infinite pieces.

Every single second from that moment was painful for him. He went down with tears in his eyes.

That night, the moon looks drowning in the sky, and stars are fading away; heartaches and time slow down... every moment feels heavy.

CHAPTER SIXTEEN

MOVING ON: A SCAM

Not knowing what to do anymore, Samir decided to share with his friends while protecting Gunika's identity, so he made up his story without letting anyone know about Gunika.

He called and asked his friends; all of them suggested moving on, and he also thought of doing so at some point.

For the next month, Samir focused on himself, as Gunika was not going to talk with him for some time, but with time he understood one thing.

> *"Moving on is a scam, there is no such thing as moving on in real love, every single instance is now fixed for that person no other person even much better than that person comes into your life you feel nothing, but in this situation, on the thing, we all can do is cope up."*

Samir was doing the same thing as his friends told him; it was on his self-respect now to not persuade or think or talk to her. But if you have been in love with someone you know and understand, one thing that goes into your mind is

"Just once more, keep my self-respect and ego aside, maybe he or she will come back and understand my worth and feelings and in some cases, even their presence is all you need that's why you do whatever it takes to keep them in your life as you want to be there for them, especially in worst times. You can't see them cry and sad."

CHAPTER SEVENTEEN

NEW START

Samir called her with the same mindset, and he started with a general topic.

"*How's life going on?*" he asked.

"*Good, really good,*" she replied.

"*Great, I am sorry for that day and understand your point of view. It's hard for girls, and we expect that girls will just answer our questions, but girls also have to keep different things in their minds. I respect that, but can we be friends, as usual, besties?*" Samir said.

"*Yes, I understand, and thanks for your understanding. I did it for you only. Yes, we can, but please don't expect anything from my side,*" she replied.

"*Yeah, but as we were besties, we will keep that vibe, right?*" Samir asked in a low voice.

"*I don't remember since when we were besties,*" Gunika replied.

That shattered Samir's heart. Samir knew he was at fault, but more than that, he knew most of the things and present surprises he curated for her were as a best friend sincerely. As for Samir, who was from the start very introverted, friendship was very important; even though he was at fault in his mind. One thing was hitting up again and again.

When Gunika was having an issue with her male best friend, she realized that something was wrong with her friend and the way he was behaving. She took action to ask Samir for suggestions and sorted it out with her friend. Now, even though this is complex due to Samir's feelings, Samir was expecting Gunika to take some action for their friendship at least, but here Samir got a different response, which was unexpected but understandable.

"Maybe I am wrong, as I did so many things wrong," Samir murmured in his mind.

With a heavy heart but laughing, he didn't want to make things more awkward. Samir said, *"Yes... no problem."*.

And that's how their new friendships started.

CHAPTER EIGHTEEN

LOVE STILL GOES ON

Even though Samir was happy, he was not his usual self as he got a setback from the statement; he was very hurt, but he never showed this side to anyone.

Now Samir himself tried to forget about feelings as it was for Gunika; he didn't want to make her awkward, and he wanted to stay with her, for her, even though he knew Gunika was self-sufficient, but he wanted to be there.

But here he wants to keep his calm and doesn't want to create any issue further for her.

He knew he wouldn't be able to forget about his feelings, so he should control them, and for that, he made sure to call her very few times to check on her.

To make sure he didn't come in her way or hurt her or make her more uncomfortable, he always stayed on the sidelines to check if she was doing okay; it was hurtful but was necessary as he promised her he wouldn't repeat the same thing.

"When you want to hug that person, protect that person from all worries, you have fallen deep in

that person's love and you want to make sure he or she is doing well, but you can't do it for some reason, that's when you will feel emptiness."

The same thing was going on in the case of Samir; in addition to these things, there was one more reason why Samir didn't want to get close, as Samir wasn't sure if her family would approve of him due to his status and class.

It's common at this time to think about these pragmatic questions. The same was true for Samir.

Samir continued to talk to her while working on his priorities, but every single time he closed his eyes, he always thought about her and prayed for her health. With this, he assures himself that she is doing well and asks her once in a while how she is doing.

"At some point in time, even the most pragmatic person doesn't know what's going on. We all are fighting for something or someone, some goal, some of us for all of them family, love money, and fame. But no one of us truly knows if this task or action we are taking is enough. If you are thinking the same then you are not alone we all are into this together, all we have to do is take small steps and move forward and you will unveil the path."

CHAPTER NINETEEN

RECENT MEET-UP

In the year 2024 End, Samir got his new job, a nice-paying job. He was happy for his family as he could support them more, plan all other priorities, and most importantly, Gunika.

In the past months, Samir has always tried to keep his heart close and not go in any love angle, saying no to all those things, but one thing hasn't changed: his feelings for Gunika. He always kept it to himself, not wanting someone to peek but also wanting to tell her how much he loved her but he didn't do that as he didn't want to hurt her. Even though Samir didn't know what was going on in Gunika's mind, he was sure about one thing: *"I won't hurt her anymore and not let anyone hurt her too, even though after this much time, my feelings for her are still the same, aha..."* Samir murmured.

Samir, on the last day of his current job, for submission of all company properties and formalities, went to the office as he was working from home that week.

He called Gunika and told her about the news, and he was visiting, Gunika was happy to hear that and wanted to meet him.

"She is always like that... that's what I love about her. We are now good friends. I wanted to tell her that there is not a single day when I wasn't thinking about her... but... " Samir stopped thinking about it and slept.

The next day, Samir completed all formalities and planned the meeting with Gunika for the next day.

The next day, Samir was excited but also nervous, for a long time since that talk with Gunika, he had closed himself off a lot, but he knew that in front of Gunika, he was vulnerable; he was his true self and couldn't help it.

They met at a restaurant; as Christmas was near, it had a Christmas theme, but due to a long waiting list, they decided to look for another restaurant.

After a long search, they found a restaurant and enjoyed their conversation.

After the meetup, Samir was going back on the train, but he was not alone; with tears in his eyes and with a thought, suddenly he said to himself, *"I want to hug you, tell you how much I love you, but I am bound with these chains of promise to not hurt you and chains of status."*

In that journey, Samir wasn't happy about his new job, nice income, and all other stuff; he was feeling empty, missing his part, though he didn't mention anything in front of her, thinking he might hurt her, and he doesn't want to hurt or impose himself onto her.

> **"*Sometimes I even don't know what to say, I don't want to hurt her but want to make her realize how much she means to me, how much I care for her and love her.*"**

On the way back to his home, Samir read something powerful.

"If a person wants you in life he or she will make an effort and if he or she is truly yours that person will make it happen regardless of what circumstances are."

With that thought in mind, Samir reached his destination, and after this journey, he was sure he wouldn't be able to forget her, she was the one and would be the one always, and he would try his best till the end. With this, he begins his new journey where he is sure about his love and now .. new journey begins, whose end no one knows... till next time...

Thanks Giving

Thanks for your patience.

"A one-sided relationship is also a relationship even more than that as you will put more effort into making other people see your efforts and sincerity and loving selflessly. It's a pure memory and feeling."

To Gunika

Thanks for reading all these memories that we share. I apologise again for all the things I did, and yeah, I love you; you don't have to answer that. I am sorry if I could not capture your feelings well, as this is a one-sided story. I don't know when you will be reading this; I am not sure if I will be publishing it or not, but when it is, I will be sending you a copy, as you should know. How big of a fool Samir is for Gunika; it sounds cheesy. I know you don't like cheesy things, but it's true. I know you are the best person I have fallen for, and no one can replace you. I will always be there for you. I am not sure what to write, as while writing this, I am still teary. I hope when you are reading this, you are not mad at me. I have fulfilled my promise too, and I am trying my best to contain these feelings, and I again and every single time will say this: "I love you", and don't be mad at me; I am sorry again, as my intention wasn't to hurt you with this or make you awkward, as you know every time I do something opposite happen... hehe... Till the last moment, I won't give up, and some part of mine will always be there for you. If you are married, I hope you are happy. "Stay smiling, as it suits you more, gorgeous." I can't express my whole feelings here, you know I am very quirky always... Truly there for you every time. Signing off, Samir...

To All Gunika And Samir Out There

Firstly, thanks for reading this small story. I know the story might be different, but most of the emotions will be the same. I want to request you to please give each other a chance. **And if someone is coming back again and again to you and feels the same after so long, it doesn't mean he or she is not having self-respect or self-worth; it can also be that that person loves you a lot, and it's not a weak nature; it's a strength.** And hey Samir, yes, you who are reading, if you are a Samir, worry not; all those tears show your sincerity, not a weakness. If other person don't understand your worth don't beg it's their loss. Men only cry for women they truly love, and Gunika, yes, you, try to give Samir a chance; maybe it can be fruitful, and both of you don't include any other person in your relationship, as people usually tend to break instead of build things. All the best... signing off... Samir.

9 798896 732020